For Erin Murphy, rock star of an agent

—A. V.

For Jonathan, my rock star

—K. E.

Text copyright © 2012 by Audrey Vernick
Illustrations copyright © 2012 by Kirstie Edmunds

First published in the United States of America in February 2012
by Walker Publishing Company, Inc., a division of Bloomsbury Publishing, Inc.
www.bloomsburykids.com

For information about permission to reproduce selections from this book, write to
Permissions, Walker BFYR, 175 Fifth Avenue, New York, New York 10010

Library of Congress Cataloging-in-Publication Data
Vernick, Audrey.
    So you want to be a rock star / by Audrey Vernick ; illustrated by Kirstie Edmunds.
        p.   cm.
    Summary: Presents advice for budding rock stars, including how to strum an air guitar,
        how to sneer, and how to sign autographs.
    ISBN 978-0-8027-2092-4 (hardcover) • ISBN 978-0-8027-2325-3 (reinforced)
    [1. Rock music—Fiction. 2. Musicians—Fiction. 3. Humorous stories.] I. Edmunds, Kirstie, ill. II. Title.
    PZ7.V5973So 2012   [E]—dc22   2010048278

Art created using pencil and then painted digitally
Typeset in Bernhard Gothic Std
Book design by Regina Roff

Printed in China by C&C Offset Printing Co., Ltd., Shenzhen, Guangdong
(hardcover) 10 9 8 7 6 5 4 3 2
(reinforced) 10 9 8 7 6 5 4 3 2 1

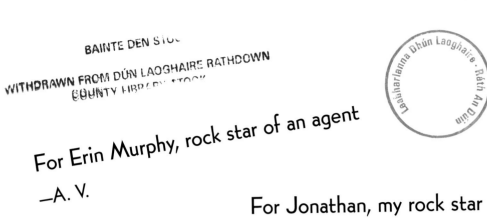

So You Want to Be a Rock Star

Audrey Vernick

illustrated by Kirstie Edmunds

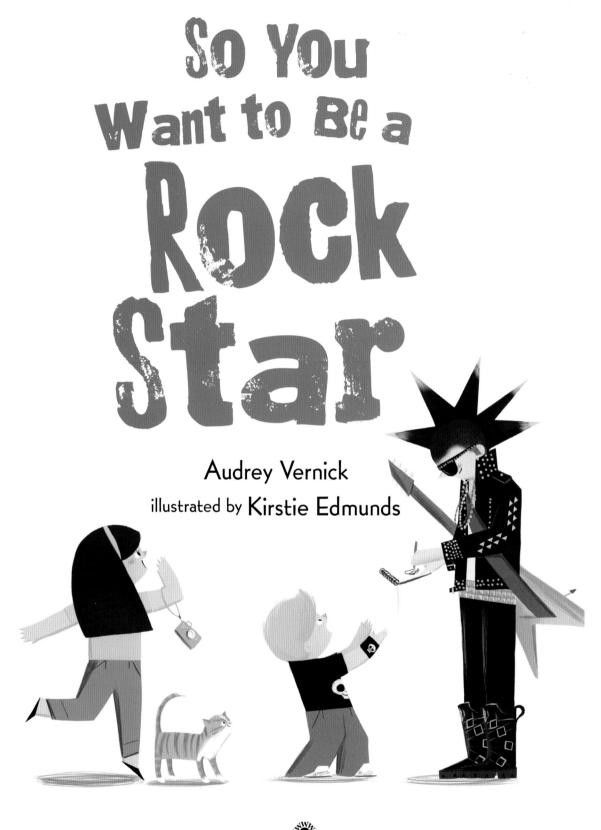

Walker & Company New York

You want to be a rock star?
Let's see if you have what it takes.

Do you have an awesome sound system
with cordless microphones?

Oh.

Well, can you make your hand into a fist
and sing into that?
Try it.

Terrific!

Do you have a really **cool** electric guitar?

That's okay.

Can you hold your left hand out to the side
and strum your stomach with your right hand?

Give it a try.

This is very important: while you're
strumming your stomach, can you also
close your eyes and make the kind of
faces you make when your stomach really
hurts? And move your head slowly from
side to side?

Try it now.

Check you out! You're so good at this.

Oh, wait.

Are you a great singer?

Hmm.

When you open your mouth and try to sing,
does a song come out?
Your voice doesn't need to be perfect.
Just really loud.

Do you know what a sneer is?
It's like a real tough-guy smile.
Can you sneer?
Look in the mirror.

You might be the

Next
Big
Thing.

Now we're getting to advanced techniques.

Can you act like a rock star in one spot, then run across the stage and act like a rock star over there?

Maybe even stand next to another person who's acting like a rock star too?

Get someone to try it with you.
How hot are you?

One thing rock stars like to do is yell
to the audience.

Shout the name of your town, and then say,
"Are you ready to **rock**?"

Imagine the crowd roaring back at you.
Fun, right?

Rock stars need to stand out
from the crowd.

Do you have awesome-crazy clothes?
Can you borrow some?

Do you have awesome-crazy hair?

Can you borrow some?

You need to make some decisions about your concerts and music videos.

Are you the kind of rock star who has dancers on stage?

If you are, hire some.

Or teach everyone in your family how to dance.

Start now.

Do you have a website?
And a huge fan club?

How about a limousine?
No? That's okay.
Do you have a driver?

Wow. Who's cooler than you?

ON AIR
REHEARSAL

Applause!

HELLO AND WELCOME TO ROCK TV

CAM 4

ROCK TV

You may end up with your own TV show.

You should probably start thinking about your theme song.
One snappy idea is to sing your first and last name four times,
starting quietly and getting louder each time.

Let's hear it!

Make sure your theme song rocks.
Because if there's a you-movie,
you'll be hearing it a lot.

And if amusement parks add you-rides, well, WOW.

Of course, whenever you leave your home, you'll be mobbed by fans.

Come up with a fast way to sign your name,
because all those fans will want your autograph.

Try it!

what?

Oh well, I'm sure you'll master cursive soon.

And then you'll be the **biggest rock star ever.**

(Until then, a fancy squiggle might be just the thing.)